A Treasury of
Curious George

A Treasury of
Curious George

Margret *and* H. A. Rey

Illustrated in the style of H. A. Rey by Vipah Interactive and Martha Weston

Houghton Mifflin Harcourt   Boston

Curious George Takes a Train © 2002 by Houghton Mifflin Company
Curious George Visits a Toy Store © 2002 by Houghton Mifflin Company
Curious George and the Dump Truck © 1999 by Houghton Mifflin Company
Curious George and the Birthday Surprise © 2003 Houghton Mifflin Company
Curious George Goes Camping © 1999 by Houghton Mifflin Company
Curious George Goes to a Costume Party © 2001 by Houghton Mifflin Company
Curious George Visits the Library © 2003 by Houghton Mifflin Company
Curious George in the Big City © 2001 by Houghton Mifflin Company

Based on the character of Curious George ®, created by Margret and H. A. Rey.
Curious George ® is a registered trademark of Houghton Mifflin Company.

Curious George and the Dump Truck and *Curious George Goes Camping* illustrated by Vipah Interactive, Wellesley, Massachusetts: C. Becker, D. Fakkel, M. Jensen, S. SanGiacomo, C. Witte, C. Yu.

Remaining selections illustrated by Martha Weston.

ISBN 978-1-328-90514-7
Manufactured in China

SCP 10 9 8 7 6 5 4 3
4500689447

A Treasury of
Curious George

Contents

MARGRET & H.A. REY'S
Curious George
Takes a Train

Illustrated in the style of H. A. Rey by Martha Weston

Houghton Mifflin Harcourt   Boston

This is George.

He was a good little monkey and always very curious.

This morning George and the man with the yellow hat were at the train station.

They were taking a trip to the country with their friend,
Mrs. Needleman. But first they had to get tickets.

Inside the station everyone was in a hurry. People rushed
to buy newspapers to read and treats to eat. Then they
rushed to catch their trains.

But one little boy with a brand-new toy engine was not in a hurry. Nor was the small crowd next to him. They were just standing in one spot looking up. George looked up, too.

NEW CITY	6:30 AM	8	OVERDALE	6:15	M	2
HILLTOP	7:00 AM		LBURG	7:25 0	M	7
OVERDALE	7:15 AM		CITY	7:50	M	6
SMALLBURG	7:45 AM		G C	8:08	M	3
BIG CITY	8:00 AM		TON	8:15	M	5
MIDDLETON	8:02 A		WNSVILLE	8:40	M	2
OLD TOWN	8:45 AM		ILL TOP	9:25	M	1
TOWNSVILLE	9:10 AM		OLD TOWN	9:55	M	8

A trainmaster was moving numbers and letters on a big sign.
Soon the trainmaster was called away. But his job did not look
finished. George was curious. Could he help?

George climbed up in a flash.

Then, just like the trainmaster,
he picked a letter off the sign and
put it in a different place.

| ARRIVALS | | | | | DEPARTURES | | | | |
CITY	TIME			TRACK	CITY	TIME			TRACK
NEW CITY	6	30	AM	8	OVERDALE	6	15	AM	2
HILLTOP	7	00	AM	3	SMALLBURG	7	25	AM	7
OVERDALE	7	15	AM	4	NEW CITY	7	50	AM	6
SMALLBURG	7	45	AM		CITY	8	08	AM	3
BIG CITY	8	00	AM		MIDDLETON	8	15	AM	5
MIDDLETON	8	02	AM		TOWNSVILLE	8	40	AM	2
OLD TOWN	A	45	AM	2	HILLTOP	9	25	AM	1
TOWNSVILLE	9	10	AM	5	OLD TOWN	9	55	AM	8

Next he took the number 9 and put it near a 2.
George moved more letters and more numbers.
He was glad to be such a big help.

"Hey," yelled a man from below. "I can't tell when my train leaves!"

"What track is my train on?" asked another man.

"What's that monkey doing up there?" demanded a woman. She did not sound happy.

OVERDALE	6:0	A M 2
SMALLBURG	7:	5 O M
NEWCITY	7: 8	A
B	8	6 3
D	N A M 5	1
T SVILLE	: A 8	M 2
LLTOP	9 25	A W 1
OLD TOWN	: 5	A 9 8

The trainmaster did not sound happy either: "Come down from there right now!" he hollered at George.

Poor George. It's too easy for a monkey to get into trouble. But, lucky for George, it's also easy for a monkey to get out of trouble.

Right then the conductor shouted, "All aboard!"

A crowd of people rushed toward the train. George simply slid down a pole,

scurried over a suitcase, and squeezed with the crowd through the gate. There he found the perfect hiding place for a monkey.

The little boy with the toy engine also ran through the gate.

"Look, Daddy," he said, "a train!"

His father looked up. "Come back, son," he yelled. "That's not our train!"

But it was too late. The
gate locked behind him.

The boy began to cry.

George peeked out
of his hiding place.

He saw the boy's toy
roll toward the tracks.
The boy ran after it.

17

This time George knew he could help.
He leaped out of his hiding place and ran
fast. George grabbed the toy engine before
the little boy came too close to the tracks.

What a close call!

When the trainmaster opened the
gate, the boy's father ran to his son.
The boy was not crying now.
He was playing with his new friend.

"So, there you are," said the trainmaster when he saw George. "You sure made a lot of trouble on the big board!"

"Please don't be upset with him," said the boy's father. "He saved my son."

The people on the platform agreed. They had seen what had happened, and they clapped and cheered. George was a hero!

Just then the man with the yellow hat arrived with Mrs. Needleman. "It's time to go, George," he said. "Here comes our train."

"This is our train, too," the father said. The little boy was excited. "Can George ride with us?" he asked.

That sounded like a good idea to everyone. So the trainmaster asked the conductor to find them a special seat.

And he did.
Right up front.

The end.

24

MARGRET & H.A. REY'S
Curious George
Visits a Toy Store

Illustrated in the style of H. A. Rey by Martha Weston

Houghton Mifflin Harcourt   Boston

This is George.

He was a good little monkey and always very curious.

Today was the opening of a brand-new toy store. George
and the man with the yellow hat did not want to be late.

When they arrived, the line to go inside wound all the way around the corner. When a line is this long, it's not easy for a

little monkey to be patient. George sneaked through the crowd.
All he wanted was a peek inside.

29

George got to the door just as the owner opened it.
"This is no place for a monkey," she said.

But George was so excited he was already inside!
Balls, dolls, bicycles, and games filled the shelves.

There were so many toys —

George didn't even know
how some of them worked.

32

And how about these hoops?
What did they do?

George was curious. He climbed
up to pull one out of the pile.
It would not move.
George pulled harder.
Still it wouldn't move.
George pulled with all fours.

Suddenly there was a terrible crash.

Red, blue, green, and yellow hoops bounced up and down and everywhere.

"Look!" exclaimed a boy, bouncing up and down himself.

"Why, I haven't seen one of these in years!" said the boy's grandmother.

She put a hoop around her waist and gave it a spin.
George tried the hula hoop, too!

Then George pretended to be a wheel.

He rolled and rolled and....

Oops! He rolled right into the owner.

The owner shook her head. "I knew you were trouble," she said. "Now you've made a mess of my new store."

Again she tried to stop George.

And again George was too quick.

In only a second he was around the corner and on the highest shelf.

Below him, George saw a
little girl point to a toy out of
reach. "Mommy, can we get that dinosaur?" she asked.

George picked up the dinosaur
and lowered it to the girl.

She was delighted. So was the
small boy next to her. "Could

you get that ball for me, please?"
he asked George.

George reached up, grabbed the
ball, and bounced it to the boy.

"May I have that puppet way over there?" asked another girl.

42

How lucky that George was a monkey! He swung off the shelf, hung on to a light, picked up the puppet, and put it right into her hands.

"What a show!" shouted a boy.
The children held up their new toys
and cheered. What a commotion!

Immediately the owner came running,
and then came the man with the yellow hat.
  "I think we've had enough
monkey business for one day,"
the owner frowned.

Just then a girl got in the long line to pay. "What a great store," she said. "What a great idea to have a little monkey helping you," her father told the owner.

"I guess you're right," the owner replied, and smiled. Then she gave George a special surprise.

"Thank you, George," she said. "My grand opening is a success because of you. Perhaps monkey business is the best business after all."

The end.

MARGRET & H.A.REY'S
Curious George
and the Dump Truck

Illustrated in the style of H. A. Rey by Vipah Interactive

Houghton Mifflin Harcourt   Boston

This is George.

He lived with his friend, the man with the yellow hat.

He was a good little monkey and always very curious.

This morning George was playing with his toys when he heard a funny noise outside his window.

It sounded like a QUACK.
George was curious. What could be
quacking underneath his window?

It was a duck, of course!
Then George heard another QUACK—and another.

Why, it was not just one duck — it was a mother duck and five small ducklings.

Ducklings were something new to George. How funny they were!

He watched the ducklings waddle after their mother. Where were they going?

George was not curious for long...

Soon he was waddling
after Mother Duck, too!

Now he could see where
they were going.

The ducks waddled all the way to the park. George loved the park. Today he saw children flying kites and gardeners planting trees by the pond. Then George saw something he had never seen in the park before.

It was a dump truck.
And it was *big*—in fact,
George was not even as
tall as one wheel!

George forgot all
about the ducklings and
stopped to look.

It would be fun to sit in such
a big truck, thought George.

No one was inside the truck.
And the window was wide open.
George could not resist.

But sitting in a big
truck was not so fun for
a little monkey after all.
George could not even
see out the window.

He was too small.
If only there were something
to climb on.

Would this make a good step
for a monkey?

It did! Now George could see out the window. He saw grass and trees and a family eating a picnic. Suddenly George heard a low rumbling sound. Was it his stomach rumbling? he wondered. (It had been a long time since breakfast.)

But the rumbling was not coming from George's stomach...

It was coming from the back of the truck! George was curious. He climbed out of the window. Then, like only a monkey can, he swung

up to the top of the truck.
Now he could take a look.
He saw the truck was filled
with dirt.

George was excited.
What could be better than
a truck full of dirt?

George jumped right in the
middle of it. Sitting on top of
the dirt, George felt the truck
bed begin to tilt...

It tilted higher and higher. The dirt began to slide. It was sliding right into the pond—and George slid with it. George was having fun.

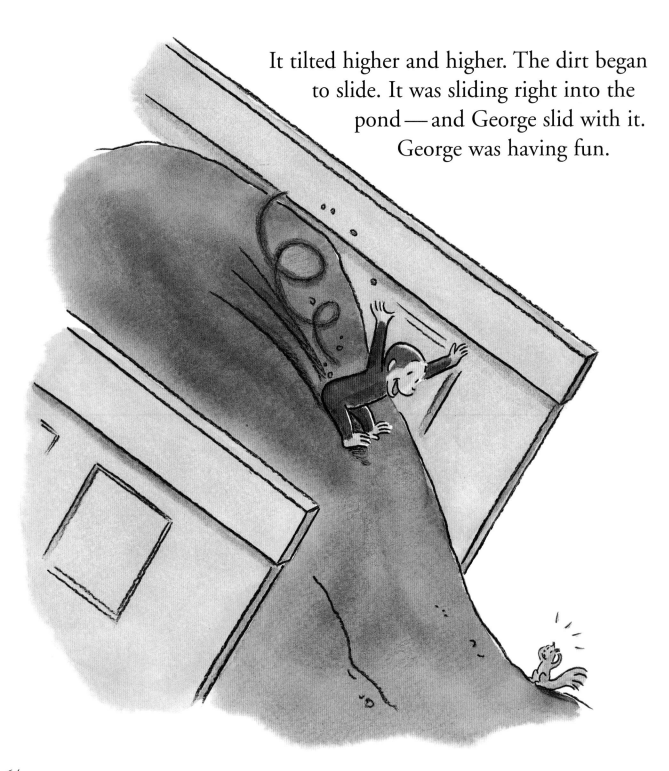

But the pile in the pond got bigger

and bigger

and BIGGER.

And soon the fun was gone.

Just then the gardeners came back from lunch and stood with their mouths wide open.

They saw the empty dump truck, the pile of dirt in the pond, and a very muddy monkey.

They knew just what had happened.

But before they could say a word, George heard a familiar sound.

He heard more quacking.
The gardeners heard it, too.
Then they heard people laughing.
"Look!" said a girl. "The ducks
have their own island!"

Indeed they did. The pile of dirt made an island in the pond — and Mother Duck and all her ducklings were waddling right on top.

George was sorry he had made such a mess, but the gardeners didn't seem to mind. "We were planting more trees and flowers to make the park nicer for people," said one of the gardeners. "But you've made the park nicer for ducks, too."

Later a small crowd gathered at the pond. "Would you like to help me feed the ducks?" a girl asked George. George was delighted. Soon everyone was enjoying the park more than ever before, including the ducks, who were the happiest of all in their new home.

The end.

MARGRET & H.A. REY'S
Curious George
and the Birthday Surprise

Illustrated in the style of H. A. Rey by Martha Weston

Houghton Mifflin Harcourt   Boston

This is George. He was a good little monkey and always very curious.

"Today is a special day," the man with the yellow hat told George at breakfast. "I have a surprise planned and lots to do to get ready. You can help me by staying out of trouble."

George was happy to help.

Later, while George was looking out the window (and being very good), he heard some tinkly music. It was coming from an ice cream truck! George watched as a whole line of children and their dogs enjoyed some ice cream treats. It looked like fun.

But when the ice cream truck moved on, George forgot all about
staying out of trouble and went to find some fun of his own.

In the living room
George found
noisemakers . . .

and hats . . .

and games!

Could this be part of
his friend's surprise?

Before George could find
out, he spotted some streamers,
balloons, and colored tissue. He
could not resist. . . .

79

Decorating was easy
for a little monkey!

Still, George was curious about the surprise.
And what was that good smell coming from
the kitchen? George followed his nose.

Mmmm. It was a cake! And it looked as good as it smelled. All it needed was frosting. George had seen his friend make frosting before.

But today his friend was busy.
Maybe George could help.
He could frost the cake himself!

First George put a bit of this in the mixing bowl.
Next he added a bit of that.
Then he turned the mixer on.

The frosting whirled
around and around.

It was whirling too fast! But when George
tried to stop the mixer it only went faster

and faster

and FASTER!

George lifted the beaters out of the bowl. Frosting flew everywhere!

Poor George. He did not mean to make such a mess. He had only wanted to help. Now how could he clean up the sticky kitchen?

Just then George heard the tinkly music again. The ice cream truck was coming back up the street, and George had an idea. Quickly he opened the door . . .

and invited all of the dogs in for a treat!

In no time, the kitchen was as clean as a whistle.

When the dogs finished
their snack George took them
back outside. The ice cream
truck was still there.
And so was his friend!

"George!" said the man with the yellow hat. "I've been looking for you. It's time for the surprise!"

George had found hats, games, decorations, and a cake.

He was curious.

Was the surprise a party?

Yes! It was a party!
George was happy to see all of his friends.
They were glad to see George, too.
"What great decorations," Bill said.
"What a lot of presents!" said Betsy.

"Why don't you play some games with the guests, George?" the man with the yellow hat suggested. "I have one more thing to do."

When George's friend came back he was carrying a cake covered in candles. This wasn't just any party. It was a birthday party! But George was *still* curious. Whose birthday was it? He watched to see who would blow out the candles.

The man with the yellow hat put the cake down right in front of George. *That* was a surprise! It was *George's* birthday. The party was for him!

Everyone sang "Happy Birthday."

Then George took a deep breath . . .

and made a wish.

"Happy Birthday, George!"

MARGRET & H.A. REY'S

Curious George

Goes Camping

Illustrated in the style of H. A. Rey by Vipah Interactive

Houghton Mifflin Harcourt   Boston

This is George.

He was a good little monkey, and always very curious.

This weekend George and his friend, the man with the yellow hat, had special plans. They were going camping!

At the campsite the man with the yellow hat unpacked their gear while George looked at all the tents. He saw tents for big families and

one just the right size for a puppy. There were even tents on wheels!

"Would you like to help me put up our tent, George?" the man asked.

George was happy to help. It would not be hard to set up a tent, he thought.

But it wasn't easy!

"George, why don't you fill our bucket with water at the pump?" his friend suggested. "We'll need it by our campfire later, when we roast marshmallows."

Mmm, marshmallows.
George loved marshmallows.
He couldn't wait to try them
roasted!

"Now don't wander off
and get into trouble," the
man warned. But George
did not hear him. He was
already gone.

At the pump George worked the handle up and down. Soon his bucket was full. On the way back down the trail, he saw a family packing up.

George watched a girl pour her bucket of water on a campfire.
The fire sizzled out.
George thought that looked like fun!

He poured his
bucket of water on
the next campfire.

"Hey," yelled a
camper. "We weren't finished
with that yet!" The camper began to chase George. But George didn't
mean to cause trouble. Now he only wanted to hide. He ran into the
forest as fast as he could, but the camper's footsteps followed close
behind. George ran faster and faster. The footsteps came closer and
closer until, suddenly,

they were passing George. Why, it was not the camper chasing George now. It was a deer! What fun to run with a deer! Forgetting all about the camper and the marshmallows, George ran after the deer. But a little monkey cannot run as fast as a deer in the woods. Before long

George was lost and all alone. He felt tired and stopped to rest. At first he was worried—he was very far from camp. But there were lots

of other animals to keep him company. He saw a lizard sunning on a rock and a squirrel chattering in a tree. Then he saw the tail of a black

and white kitty peeking out from under a bush. He was curious.
Would the kitty like to play? George gently pulled the kitty out . . .

But it was NOT a kitty!

It was a skunk — and it was scared. The skunk lifted its tail and sprayed.

WHEW! The spray smelled awful. The animals tried to get away. George wanted to get away, too. But he could not — the smell was all over him!

How would he ever get rid of
this awful smell? he wondered.

Too bad he could not take a bath
in the woods...

Then George had an idea. He could wash the smell off in the creek! George jumped into the cold water.

He splashed and scrubbed. But he was still smelly. And now he was wet, too.

But what could he do? George thought and thought. If he climbed up a tree to dry off, would the smell blow away?

No. Even dry and high up in the tree, George did not smell better.
Poor George. He wished he hadn't wandered so far from camp. He
wished he were roasting marshmallows with his friend. Suddenly
George heard footsteps heading toward him. Someone was coming!

It was the
forest animals!
But they ran right
by him. They had seen
something scary. And George
saw it, too. It was a fire!

George had gotten into trouble for putting
out one fire, but this fire wasn't in the campground...

This was an emergency!
Quickly, George climbed
down the tree and grabbed
his bucket. He scooped it full
of water in the creek.

Then — being careful not to spill — he
climbed back up and swung from branch
to branch through the trees.

When George got close enough to the fire, he reached down and poured the water on the flames. Out went the fire with a big hiss! Just then George's friend rushed out of the forest with a ranger.

"George," he called, "I was afraid you would be here."

"It's a good thing you *were* here, George," the ranger said. "We saw smoke from the campground, but you put this fire out just in time."

George was glad to help. And the man with the yellow hat was glad to see that George was safe. But he had a funny look on his face.

"George," he asked, "what is that smell?"

Back at the campsite, George's friend helped him get rid of the awful smell. After a strange bath in tomato juice, George smelled fine.

Then the man with the yellow hat invited the ranger to cook dinner with them over their own small campfire.

"Fires can be nice, if you're careful," said the ranger.

George agreed.

Especially for roasting marshmallows.

MARGRET & H.A. REY'S
Curious George
Goes to a Costume Party

Illustrated in the style of H. A. Rey by Martha Weston

Houghton Mifflin Harcourt   Boston

This is George.

He was a good little monkey and always very curious.

One day George and his friend, the man with the yellow hat, were on their way to a party at Mrs. Gray's house.

George could not wait. He liked parties, and he was looking forward to seeing Mrs. Gray. But when the door opened George did not see Mrs. Gray at all — he saw a witch!

"Don't be afraid, George," said the man with the yellow hat. "This witch is our friend."

The witch took off her mask. It was Mrs. Gray after all! "Oh dear," she said, "did I forget to tell you this was a costume party?"

George had never been to a costume party before. Inside he saw
more people that he knew. They were all wearing costumes. There was
his friend Betsy dressed up like an astronaut. And was that Bill? Why,
he looked just like a mummy!

George wanted to wear a costume, too.
"I have some dress-up clothes upstairs,"
said Mrs. Gray. "Would you like to
use them to make a costume, George?"

Mrs. Gray took George to
a room with a big trunk filled
with clothes.

"Borrow anything you like,
George," she said. "I have
just the thing for your friend
downstairs."

George tried on lots of costumes.

The first was too big.

The next was too small.

Another was too silly.

And this one was too scary!

At last George found a costume that was just right. George was a rodeo cowboy! He wore a vest and pants with fringe. He even had a lasso and a hat!

If only he could see himself in the mirror.

George was curious. Could he see himself if he stood on the bed?

No. He needed to jump higher.

George bounced on the bed — just a little — but still he couldn't see.

He bounced a little more, and a little more.

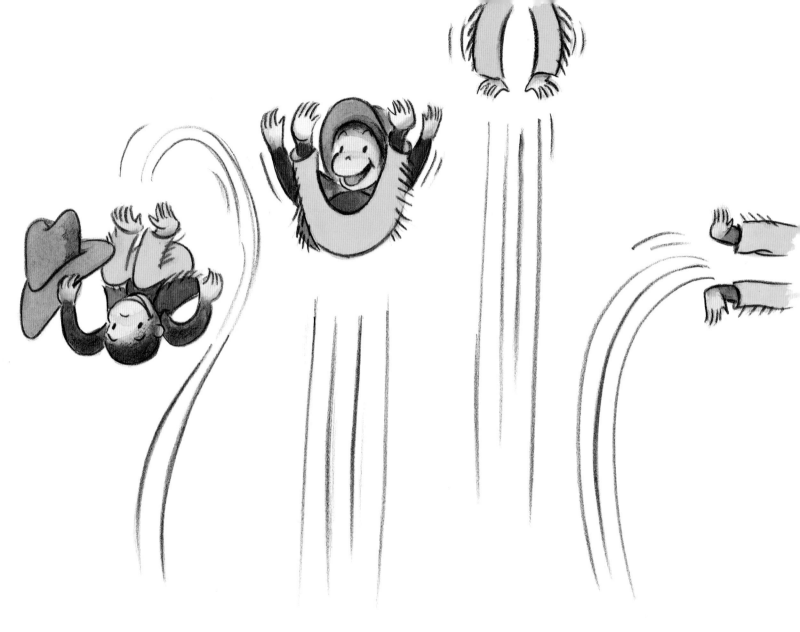

Soon George was having so much fun he forgot all about looking
in the mirror. He bounced as high as he could until—

CRASH!—George bounced off the bed.
He smashed into the night table and
got tangled up in the tablecloth.
Suddenly everything went dark.

George heard the people
downstairs gasp, "What
was that?"
"Was that a ghost?"

A ghost?! George did not want to meet up with a ghost alone. He dashed out of the room and down the hall. He wanted to get back to his friend in a hurry and he knew the fastest way.

He hopped onto the
stair rail and sailed —
WHOOSH! — down
the stairs.

"It *is* a ghost!" someone screamed. Everyone turned. They looked scared, and they were looking at George. The ghost must be right behind him!

George flew off the rail and landed—PLOP!—in the arms of a farmer. But this wasn't really a farmer. It was his friend, the man with the yellow hat!

Soon everyone stopped looking scared and started to laugh.

"That's not a ghost. That's a cowboy!" laughed a policeman.
"That's not a cowboy. That's a monkey!" giggled a princess.
"That's not just any monkey," said Betsy. "It's Curious George!"
Everyone clapped and cheered. They liked George's Halloween trick.

"You gave us a good scare, George," said Mrs. Gray. "And I'm glad to see you found some interesting costumes. Now why don't I take your ghost outfit so you can join the party?"

After the guests bobbed for apples, lit jack-o'-lanterns, and played some party games, prizes for the best costumes were handed out.

There was one prize for Betsy, and one
for Bill, and *two* for Curious George.

"You were the best ghost *and* the best cowboy, George," said Mrs. Gray.

Everyone had a good time at the party, especially George.
Too soon it was time to say goodbye.

"Good night, George."
Happy Halloween!

MARGRET & H.A.REY'S

Curious George

Visits the Library

Illustrated in the style of H. A. Rey by Martha Weston

Houghton Mifflin Harcourt   Boston

This is George.

He was a good little monkey and always very curious.

Today George and his friend the man with the yellow hat were at the library.

George had never been to the library before. He had never seen so many books before, either. Everywhere he looked, people were reading.

Some people read quietly to themselves.

But in the children's room the librarian was reading out loud.

It was story hour!

George loved stories. He sat down with a group of children to listen.

The librarian was reading a book about a bunny.

George liked bunnies.

Behind the librarian was a book about a dinosaur. George liked dinosaurs even more. He hoped she would read it next.

But next the librarian read a book about a train.

George tried to sit quietly and wait for the dinosaur book to be read.

But sometimes it is hard for a little monkey to be patient.

When the librarian started a story about jungle animals, George could not wait any longer. He had to see the dinosaur book.

He tiptoed closer.

"Look, a monkey!" shouted a girl.

The librarian put her finger to her lips. "We must be quiet so everyone can hear," she said nicely.

"But there's a monkey!" said a boy.

The librarian nodded and smiled. "Mmm-hmm," she agreed.

When she finished reading the jungle story,
the librarian reached for the dinosaur book.
Where did it go?
And where was George?

George was all ready to take the dinosaur book home and read it with his friend when another book caught his eye . . .

This book was about trucks.
George wanted to take it home, too!
And here was a book about elephants.
George loved elephants. He added it to his pile.

George found so many good books, he soon had more than he could carry. He leaned against a shelf to rest.

Squeak, went the shelf.

"Shhh!" said a man.

Squeak, went the shelf again—and it moved! Why, it wasn't really a shelf after all. George had found a special cart for carrying books.

What luck! Now George could carry all the books he wanted.
He rolled the cart between the shelves and stacked up books
about boats and kites and baking cakes. He climbed higher to reach
books about cranes and planes.

At last George had all the books he could handle. He couldn't wait to head home and start reading. And right in front of him was a ramp leading to the door. George was curious. Could he roll the cart all the way home?

Down the ramp George went. The cart rolled faster and faster.

"Stop!" a library volunteer shouted. "Come back here with my cart!"

But George was too excited to listen. The cart was picking up speed, and George was having fun!

Until — CRASH! — George and the cart ran
smack into a shelf of encyclopedias.
Books flew up in the air.
And so did George! He landed in a big pile
right between O and P.

161

"Oh no!" moaned the volunteer when he saw the mess George had made. "How am I going to put away all of these books?"

"I'd like to borrow this one," said a boy from story hour. "And I'll take this one," said a girl.

With help from George and the children,
the books were sorted in no time. Soon there
was just a small pile of George's favorites left.

"Would you like to take those books home with you?" the volunteer asked George. Then he took George to a special desk and helped him get his very own library card.

George was holding his brand-new card when his friend arrived with a stack of books of his own. "There you are, George!" he said. "I see you are all ready to check out."

George and his friend gave their books to the librarian.

She smiled when she saw George's pile. "I was wondering where this dinosaur book went," she said. "It's one of my favorites, too."

The librarian stamped the books and handed them back to George.

With his books under one arm,
George waved goodbye to the
volunteer, the librarian, and
the children from story hour.

166

"Come see us again, George,"
the librarian said, waving back.
"Enjoy your books!"

And he did.

The end.

MARGRET & H.A. REY'S

Curious George

in the Big City

Illustrated in the style of H. A. Rey by Martha Weston

Houghton Mifflin Company   Boston

This is George.

He lived with his friend the man with the yellow hat. He was a good little monkey and always very curious.

Today George was in the big city.

"Let's stop here, George," his friend suggested. "I would like to get you a holiday surprise before we see the sights."

George loved surprises. He wanted to get a surprise for the man with the yellow hat, too. Why, here was a whole pile of surprises — all ready to go! Would one of these be right for his friend?

George was curious.

He opened a box and peeked inside. The box was empty. (That was not a good surprise!) George opened another box, and another. They were all empty!

Suddenly the store clerk came running. "Stop! Please!" he cried. "You are ruining my display!"

But George did not want to stop. He wanted to go. He wanted to get away — fast! Quickly, he climbed on the escalator. George went up. The clerk went up, too.

What George wanted now was to find his friend. What luck! George spotted a yellow hat on the escalator going down. Could that be his friend?

George wanted to find out.
Soon he was going down, too.

George followed the yellow hat out of the store and around the corner.

He chased it down some stairs. Where could his friend be going? Was this George's surprise?

No, this was the subway!

George got on the train just in time. He thought maybe his friend was playing a game with him. But where was the man now? George looked around. The train was very crowded. Could that be him on the other end of the subway car? It might be hard to get there...

but not too hard for a little monkey!

Suddenly the train stopped—and when the doors opened, the yellow hat disappeared. George followed as quickly as he could, but he was too late. This was not a surprise after all. This was a mistake. The yellow hat was nowhere to be seen. Poor George. He was all alone in the big city. How would he ever find his friend now?

Soon George could see nothing but legs. He was surrounded by a crowd of moving people, and he had to keep moving himself so that he would not get stepped on.

Then George heard a woman's voice coming from the head of the crowd. "Going up," she said.

Up! That was just what George needed. He needed to be high up, like in a tree or on the escalator. Then he could get a good look around. George joined the crowd as they got into an elevator and went up.

Here was a good lookout! From up here George could see a bridge, lots of tall buildings, and a little green lady standing in the water. But he did not see his friend.

"It's time to go," called the woman from the elevator. "We have lots more to see." The crowd followed the woman. They wanted to see more. George wanted to see more, too.

Soon George was on a big bus driving through the city.

There *was* lots more to see!

But no matter where George looked,

he did not see the man with the yellow hat.

Back on the bus, George looked and looked. Finally, he saw something familiar. George was excited. He rushed inside. He was sure to find his friend here! Instead, he ran right into the clerk.

"You're just the one I've been looking for to help me fix this mess," he said.

George felt bad. He had not meant to make such a mess.

Could he help rewrap the boxes? George took some ribbon in one hand, some paper in another, and some tape in a third.

Then, like only a monkey can, George wrapped those boxes. Soon, a crowd gathered to watch. Everyone wanted George to wrap their boxes, too.

Just as George tied his twenty-fifth quadruple bow, he spotted his friend. At last! George was happy. But when he saw that the man was carrying a present, George became sad. He had forgotten all about finding a surprise for his friend. Then he had an idea...

"George!" exclaimed the man with the yellow hat. "What a good surprise!" His friend was very glad to see him. "I've been looking all over the store for you," he said. "And now I have a surprise for you, too."

George opened his surprise and put it on.

It fit perfectly.

"Now we're ready to see the sights," the man said.

George held tightly to his friend's hand and everyone waved goodbye.

"Let's be careful not to get separated again," the man with the yellow hat said as they left the store.

"The best part of the holidays is spending time together."
George agreed.

The end.